THE ISAAC SPIDERS

ISBN 978-0-9954247-1-5

This is a work of fiction. Names, characters, businesses, places, events and incidents are either the products of the author's imagination or used in a fictitious manner. Any resemblance to actual persons, living or dead, or actual events is purely coincidental.

For contact details please visit www.Thomas-Rose.com

Dedicated to the memory of Paul

Praise for 'The Isaac Spiders' on Amazon.com

"It is a gripping tale of an unusual variety."

"At first I thought the story was progressing too slowly, but that was all part of Rose's plan."

"Rose has produced a slow-burning, climatic and atmospheric tale that lures you in gently, makes you feel at home with it's own innocuous quirkiness, and then strikes, hard, decisively, fatally. Much like a spider."

"Holds its grip until the very last page."

"The Isaac Spiders builds suspense relentlessly: slowly and surely, with cinematic scenes and one hell of a twist, which stays with you long after you finish reading."

"Intriguing, building, chilling."

THE ISAAC SPIDERS

PROLOGUE

"There it is!"

The pair stared at the decrepit house. Both were in the throes of mid-adolescence, and sweat had beaded on their pimpled foreheads on the hike from the caravan park. The more rotund of the pair was panting.

"Just like he said it was."

"Looks… spooky." Adrian said between breaths.

"I believe that's the point."

"Whatever. We going to check it out?"

Isaac gave him a look as if to say *duh* and moved for the sagging porch. Its old wooden steps protested under his feet but held. Adrian followed.

The grey wooden door still stood on rusty hinges.

"Look," Isaac pointed at something carved into the door.

A symbol had been crudely scraped into the wood. Its shape roughly resembled two overlapping right angles which formed a square in the middle. Two floating squares were nestled in the opposing outside corners, while two smaller right angles floated around the interior square. The combination of weird angles and geometry, however roughly presented, was something they had never seen before.

"Spooky," Adrian repeated.

"Do not cross here," Isaac read the words carved beneath the symbol, "Wonder what it means?"

"Maybe the place is booby trapped," Adrian said, "or haunted!"

Isaac gave him another look and pushed the door open. No hidden darts fired at them. No vengeful ghost appeared. The only thing that hit them was cool, stale air.

"Come on." Isaac stepped inside and beckoned Adrian to follow.

Inside, a narrow hallway ran from the front to the back of the house. A door matching the one they had just entered was visible at the other end. Other doorways gaped off the light starved corridor. A balustraded flight of stairs ascended into similar gloom above them. The air was surprisingly still.

"Let's check upstairs first," Isaac said.

"Those stairs don't look safe."

"You scared?"

"What? No!"

"Then come on."

They creaked and groaned, but the stairs didn't collapse.

The second floor was much like the first, except at the far end there was a boarded up window. Doorways sprouted off a central corridor. What light there was came from the half open doors.

Overcoming his trepidation, Adrian walked to the end of the second floor and disappeared into one of the rooms without Isaac.

Isaac poked his head into the closest room. Except for a large, freestanding wardrobe, it was empty. He moved to inspect the lone piece of furniture.

It had been abandoned but it was beautiful. Its dark wood was carved into swirling channels and bulges that collided and diverged with crafted elegance. Once lacquered timber was now exposed in patches but the mottled effect only added to the charm.

"Hey!" Isaac called out. "Come check this out."

Adrian appeared a few seconds later.

"Want to go to Narnia?" Isaac patted the side of the wardrobe, grinning.

"That's cool," Adrian said.

"Find anything else in the other rooms?"

"Nah, nothing in them." Adrian opened the wardrobe doors and looked inside. It was cavernous and empty. "Loads of dust. One had a broken window."

"Wanna check out downstairs?"

"Sure."

Isaac led the way back to the ground floor.

A step collapsed beneath him, sending him tumbling to the bottom. Dust erupted in a cloud around him.

"Man!" Adrian picked his friend up. "You okay?"

"Yeah, yeah… I think so." Isaac dusted himself off.

"Told you those stairs didn't look safe."

"Whatever." He rolled up his jeans and was greeted by the sight of a nasty graze.

"You can walk?"

Isaac hobbled to the rear of the house in answer. "Come on."

They peered through the various doors they passed on their way to the rear of the house. All of them were half furnished, as if the house's final occupants had started to move everything out and then decided not to bother.

"Check it out."

The rear door opened out onto a verandah, its short steps emptying onto what had once been a beautiful garden. Now it was nothing but a jungle of half-dead overgrowth.

"What's that?"

Isaac followed the line of Adrian's pointing finger to a half-hidden structure lurking beneath the overgrowth. He moved down into the feral garden and said, "Let's find out."

They tip-toed through the knee-high grass, eyes scanning for snakes. They battled several thick shrubs before coming to the structure in question: a large, squat shed made of corrugated tin. A wide doorway was filled by two metal doors, a chain and padlock holding them closed.

"It's locked."

Isaac, already fiddling with the padlock, gave Adrian another look. "You're very good at stating the obvious. Huh, this padlock looks relatively new…" He dropped the chain and pulled at one of the doors. A gap, just enough to squeeze through, appeared.

"Come on."

"You serious?"

"Of course I'm serious," Isaac said. "Let's check out inside."

"Nah man, looks dark in there. Besides…" Adrian whacked his chubby stomach.

Isaac rolled his eyes and – without saying a word – squeezed through the gap.

Adrian wasn't wrong. It was dark in here. Really dark. Isaac pulled his phone from his pocket, using its light to look around.

The shed was built on top of wood beams, and straw was littered over them. Water had seeped past the metal enclosure and the whole place smelled like damp straw. It was completely empty.

"What's in there?" Adrian's voice was muffled on the other side of the doors.

"Not much… Wait."

Isaac hobbled to the back of the shed and knelt in the straw. An old frayed rope lay on the ground. Grabbing it, he noticed that it fed into a hole in a roughly square slab of wood.

"Dude," Isaac called out to Adrian, "there's a trapdoor in here."

"Woah, cool."

Isaac pulled on the rope and the trapdoor creaked open, revealing steps that descended into blackness. He let go of the rope and the door fell on the ground with a loud BANG.

"What was that!" Adrian yelled. "You okay?"

"I'm fine," Isaac called back, "just opened the trapdoor."

"What do you see?"

"Nothing." Isaac thought for a second. "I'm going to go down and check it out."

"Be careful."

"Yes mum," Isaac said. There was no answer. That shut him up.

Isaac toggled the phone's camera to video mode. He pointed it at the gaping hole for a few seconds before climbing down, the recording still running.

The roof was low so it didn't take long for Isaac to reach the bottom. In fact, the short flight of stairs seemed unnecessary. While it would be a stretch, it would be possible to climb out of the trapdoor with nothing more than the assistance of a small stool.

"Isaac!" His anxious voice was even more muffled, but Adrian was still audible.

"I'm fine," he called back, "shut up!"

Isaac swept the view of the phone around the low vaulted space. The walls and floor were hewn from the sandstone roots of the nearby mountains. Straw had fallen through the cracks in the floor above and sat in patches amidst small pools of water with nowhere to go in this stone sealed cellar. A tall set of shelves sat on the far wall. No way that had been brought down through the trapdoor. It had to have been made down here.

Sweeping the phone's light across the beams threatening to catch his head, he noticed something. Lots of somethings. Etched into the beams and floorboards was were a swarm of symbols.

While the style of lines varied from symbol to symbol – some straight, some horribly skewed – they all matched the symbol carved into the house's front door. Touching the phone's screen, he zoomed in on a particularly dense collection of them.

"What do you see?" Adrian's voice was even more muffled now that Isaac was down in the cellar.

"You know that symbol on the front door?"

"Yeah?"

"It's all over the place down here."

"Send pics man."

Isaac took a few shots but they wouldn't send. "Can't man, no reception down here."

"Well, show me them all when you get back up here!"

Isaac returned the device to video mode and took more footage of the symbol-ridden beams before moving on towards the back of the cellar.

"There's a tunnel," Isaac said, his phone pointed in the direction of a half-hidden crack in the wall. Blackness yawned behind it.

"What?"

"I said, there's a tunnel!" Isaac shouted. He paused to think for a moment before deciding, "I'm going to check it out."

"Be careful! And take photos!"

Isaac ignored the warning and held the phone in front of him, having already decided to keep it on video mode while he explored.

Approaching the crack, it seemed like passage through it would be difficult, but the way the rock folded around itself was deceptive. Isaac managed to walk easily through the crack, his shoulders only brushing the sides. The low ceiling gained height the further he moved into the crack until it spilled out into a much larger space.

"Woah."

He found himself in middle of an old mine, wood-trussed walls disappearing to his left and right.

Pointing the phone both ways, its white light was swallowed by darkness. He looked back into the crack and called out, "Adrian!"

A thousand echoes replied but none of them were Adrian's voice.

Isaac tapped his foot for a couple of seconds, trying to decide what to do next. This place looked like it was huge and he couldn't just leave Adrian outside by himself. The guy would worry himself to death, or – worse – decide to go get their parents. Once his mother found out Isaac had been crawling around in an old mine she would freak.

Almost as if in answer, a text message managed to slip through the rock and soil above him to the screen of his phone: *Where are you boys? We're going to dinner in town soon.*

Isaac let out a sigh of disappointment. He was either going to have to come back another day or not at all.

He looked around for a souvenir of some sort. If his exploration was going to be cut short, he wanted to at least take something. Most of what lay around was rocks. Ideally, he was hoping for a small nugget of gold. This was a mine, after all. What he found instead was far more interesting.

Isaac's light caught a grey clump lying on the ground.

It was a dead spider.

The thing was lying on its back, legs curled up above it, the universal 'I'm dead' position of spiders everywhere.

Wanting to make sure, he poked it with its foot.

Yup, dead.

Isaac squatted down to have a closer look, the phone still recording.

It looked like a tarantula. Or, at least what Isaac thought of as tarantulas. He had only ever seen them pinned to boards in museums or on TV, but none of them had looked like this one. Its body bristled with ash coloured hairs mixed with pale purple flecks. Its thin legs swelled at its knees, or at least what Isaac thought were spider's knees.

"Man, this thing is freaky," Isaac muttered.

1

Its small, shiny eyes stared at him through the glass. Their pupil-less black masked its intentions. Were they set on murder? Or obsessed with a life-preserving hunger? Its thick, black legs felt their way across the mulch. Tiny hairs sensed the movement of the air as it crawled towards him, unaware of the prison that held it.

Bzzt.

The creature stopped in front of the glass, lifting its front legs above its head, touching the air. It reared itself up onto four legs and bared its fangs.

Bzzt.

It held its aggressive stance, poised to strike.

Tap.

The fangs lashed out, glancing off the glass, drops of venom beading on the invisible wall.

Tap. Tap.

Another vicious attempt to bite his finger through the glass. The venom began to drip down the surface, colouring the red mulch a dark crimson.

The call connected and Flynn turned from the terrarium, swiveling on his chair in the direction of his work station.

"Blue Mountains Caravan Park, Trisha speaking, how may I

help you?"

"Hey Trisha," Flynn toyed with a pen in front of him, "Just ringing to make an enquiry about this weekend."

"We're full up on powered sites, got a few non-powered-"

"Any cabins?" Flynn interrupted.

Trisha's fingers tapped on a keyboard, "We've got one bungalow left."

"Awesome, we'll take it."

"How many will be staying?"

"My wife and I."

"Mmmhm," more tapping, "how long?"

"The Friday through Monday. We'll clear out with the rest of the weekend crowd on Monday morning."

"Mmmhm."

"Oh…" Flynn kept his voice even, as if his next question was just an afterthought. "Do you allow dogs?"

"Only in specific areas of the park. Must be kept outside. Leashes at all times," she sounded bored as she rattled off the rules. "What sort of dog?"

"German Shepherd. Well trained. He won't be any trouble," Flynn said with rehearsed brevity.

"Shouldn't be a problem, but there's a surcharge."

"No problems. What's the damage?"

"All up, on peak for the three days and the animal surcharge, we've got…" more tapping, "Three hundred. What name am I putting that under?"

"Flynn Schilder."

"All right then, you're all booked in for arrival tomorrow, just come to the front office and we'll get you sorted."

"Thanks Trisha, we'll see you tomorrow night."

"Bye."

Flynn hung up just as his phone chimed. With a tap, he navigated to the new text message: *I'm lost. Where are you?*

Flynn called the number. It was picked up on the second ring.

"Hey!" The voice on the other end was over eager and nervous, "It's Isaac."

"Hi," Flynn said, "whereabouts are you?"

"Um… Near the café?"

"Which one?" Flynn grabbed his jacket.

"It's called Ricardo's."

"You're nowhere close. Hold tight, I'll be right there."

"Okay, see you soon."

Flynn hung up the call and shrugged into his jacket. Flipping the internal side of the lock, he left the lab for the biology building's many hallways and stairwells, eventually working his way out into the spring air.

The hour had just turned, and students were streaming out of their various classes with laptops and tablets tucked under their arms. Their chatter was filled with complaints about lecturers, assignment loads, and longings for the coming weekend.

He joined the flow of students, forced at times to skirt around slower moving clumps of smartphone wielders as he made his way to Ricardo's.

Isaac. The high schooler who believed he'd found a new species of spider and was transparently eager to prove it. That's who had been on the phone and that was who Flynn was about to meet.

At first, he had been dubious of the young teenager's claim in his initial email, but the stream of photographic evidence he sent Flynn's way was enough to pique the arachnologist's interest. While the photos had been poorly lit and grainy, there was something undeniably foreign – even alien – about the creature Isaac had found. It had been enough for Flynn to plan a trip up into the mountains to check it out for himself.

A group of students had decided to have a conversation in

the middle of a crossroad and Flynn found himself snarled in a particularly dense knot of foot traffic. Forsaking the path, he cut across a large quadrangle. A passing grounds man gave him a dirty look. Flynn ignored him and continued over the lush green grass.

He arrived outside Ricardo's and looked around. An out-of-place teenager in a blue blazer sat at a numbered table, a bag propped against his leg. He approached the boy. "Isaac?"

"Dr. Schilder?"

"Flynn," he shook the teen's extended hand and sat. "You said you had something for me?"

Isaac dug around inside his bag and produced a plastic container. He slid it across the surface of the table. Lying on the bottom was a curled up spider carcass.

"Sorry about the legs," the teen mumbled as he handed it to Flynn.

Flynn looked inside, seeing the reason for the teen's apology. All eight legs had disintegrated and lay on the bottom of the container like ash. Thick stumps were all that remained.

"Mmm," Flynn continued to turn the container in his hands, inspecting the dead creature inside.

"Is it a new species?"

"Can't tell you right now," Flynn said.

"When can you?"

Flynn took a proper look at Isaac. The teen was shifting with nervous energy and a slight sheen of sweat had broken out on his forehead.

"Sometime over the weekend."

"That long?"

"Confirming a new species takes a lot of work. Tarantulas aren't common this far south. I've got to do some research."

"Okay..." the teen sounded disappointed.

Flynn threw him a bone. "I'll let you know the moment I know. Sound good?"

"Cool."

"I'm heading up to the caravan park for the weekend to see if I can find some live specimens. That will give me a much better indication of whether or not we're dealing with a new species."

"Yeah?" He perked up a bit. "Cool."

"Can you tell me where the old house is?"

Isaac shook his head. "Not really."

"How did you and your friend find it?"

"This weird old guy in a caravan told us. You could ask him."

"That's not much information to work with," Flynn said. "Can you tell me anything about the man and his caravan? Where in the park was it? Did he give you a name?"

"No name but it was towards the rear of the caravan park, kinda tucked behind a shower block. There was a whole bunch of caravans set up there."

Retirees living on the cheap, Flynn thought.

"What colour was the caravan?" He asked.

"Green… I think."

"You think?"

"I dunno man, it was really dirty, covered in leaves and twigs. The sides looked green but who knows? I didn't exactly stop and take a picture. Speakin' of…" The teen dug around in his backpack, producing a small plastic stick. "It's got the video on it."

"Thanks." Flynn took the USB drive and put it in his pocket. "So I'm looking for an old man living in a dirty green caravan behind a shower block?"

"Yup."

"Nothing else?"

"I think he was blind…"

"What made you think that?"

"He never blinked. His eyes didn't move at all. Was kinda creepy until we realised."

"So, to revise, I'm looking for a blind old man living in a dirty green caravan behind a shower block?"

"Yup."

"You're sure that's as much as you know?"

"Yeah man."

A waitress came over to their table, put down a milkshake and picked up the table number, leaving without a word. Isaac pulled the drink towards him and started slurping on the straw.

"Alright," Flynn said, "I'm going to take this-" he tapped the container in front of him "-back to the lab and give it a look over."

Isaac stopped slurping, "And you'll let me know tonight?"

"I'll let you know when I'm sure," Flynn corrected. "That may not be until the end of the weekend, and even then… this stuff takes time."

"Just make sure no one else finds out about it."

"Why?"

"Don't want anyone stealing my discovery."

"That's not going to happen," Flynn reassured him.

"But still!"

"Fine, I'll keep it secret."

"Good." Isaac resumed slurping at his milkshake. "Also if it is a new species–"

"If," Flynn reminded him.

"Yeah," Isaac said, "if it is… can I name it?"

Flynn smiled, "Sure. What do you want to name it?"

"The Isaac Spider," the teen said simply.

"You want to name it after yourself?"

"Yeah?" he got defensive, "What's wrong with that?"

"Nothing," Flynn assured him, "It just might be better to name it something a little more… scientific."

"Hey, I discovered it, so you're naming it after me. Otherwise I'll sue you for copyright." Isaac realised that didn't sound quite right, "or something."

"The Isaac Spider," Flynn humoured him. "Got it. Now I'm going to go check this thing out back at the lab."

"Can I come?" Isaac asked.

"No," Flynn said, and left.

2

Flynn reached for his half-filled mug and raised it to his lips before lowering it in disgust. The coffee, made hours ago, was cold. He had become so absorbed in his work that he had forgotten it.

The specimen lay in front of him on a white ceramic pad. A notebook sat off to the left, black scrawl clinging to its faint blue lines. To the right was a brace of various tweezers and other finely pointed instruments that had prodded, turned, and dissected the spider for the past couple of hours. The carcass was now almost unrecognizable. But that didn't matter.

It was a new species. Flynn was sure of it.

From the unique ash grey and purple streaked colouring, to the separated cephalothorax, blunt head, complete lack of fangs and spinnerets, and the incredibly thick leg stumps, everything screamed 'new'.

There was almost nothing about it that resembled any other known spider, not once he had broken down the particulars. Its body was articulated like an ant, not a spider, and yet the presence of the eight leg stumps prevented him from ruling out an arachnid classification.

His phone buzzed once. He flipped it over, checking the message displayed on screen. It was from Steph.

Where are you?

He thumbed out a reply.

Still at the lab. Be home soon. Want me to grab dinner?

He turned his attention to his computer, its screen coated in observations, pictures, and the technobabble of a rabid arachnologist.

Steph replied a few minutes later: *Sounds great. What you thinking? Also, your latest package arrived.*

Flynn smiled: *Awesome! And dinner? Secret.*

Steph's reply: *My favourite kind. See you soon.*

Flynn finalized his notes before slapping the lid of his laptop closed. He shoved it into an open backpack along with its already bundled up charger.

Shouldering the bag, he picked his wallet and keys off the low countertop he used as a desk and headed for the door. He flipped the lab's lights off and shut the door behind him.

He rattled the keys in the lock, ensuring it was secure before walking down the hall and outside onto the wider campus grounds. His car was parked a short walk from his lab in a faculty zone: no student vehicles allowed.

Walking into the asphalt lot, he pressed a button in his pocket. The lights of a sensible, late model station wagon flashed a few vehicles down. He closed the distance, opened the door, and climbed inside. Reaching across the centre console, he placed his bag in the foot well of the passenger seat before bringing the engine to life and pulling out.

3

Flynn pulled into the driveway of an ordinary suburban home. A single Jacaranda tree rose out of the front lawn, its roots bulging up beneath a red brick path winding its way to the front entrance.

He killed the engine and collected his things, including this evening's dinner. Locking the car, he entered the house through a side door, finding himself in a recently renovated kitchen.

"Well hello."

He turned to see his wife, Steph, seated at the kitchen table. She had a stack of paper on either side of her and a red pen in hand.

"Hello yourself," Flynn said with a smile, putting the food on the bench, "What you got there?"

"What do you think?" She said, giving him a look before getting up, "Work." She put her arms around Flynn and squeezed, "Welcome home."

"Thanks." He squeezed back, looking at the stacks of paper on the table. "Finally got around to marking those essays?"

She let out an exasperated sigh and pulled away from him. "Yeah. If I have to correct one more student on the fact that Frankenstein is the doctor and not the monster, I'm going to scream."

"That's what you get for tutoring a first year Gothic literature class. Want to swap?"

She gave him daggers, "I would much rather contend with mis-labelled, fictitious monsters than big, black, dangerous spiders."

"Oh you mean Sheila?"

"Flynn! It's a funnel web! Did you really have to name it?" She said, sitting back down amongst her papers.

"I name all my spiders, you know that."

"I'm so glad I didn't let you bring that one home."

Flynn stole a glance at the kitchen counter and the box sitting on it. He had spotted the package as soon as he had walked in, but deliberately hadn't moved towards it. Steph caught him eyeing it off.

"You know, you're terribly unsubtle." She picked up the red pen again, looking down. "I've noticed every glance you've made."

He crossed to the bench and picked up the package. Unable to tear the tape with his fingers, he rummaged around the kitchen drawer.

"Do not use the steak knives," Steph said without looking up, "or…" She let her warning trail off.

Flynn pulled out the kitchen scissors and gave the air a few snips. "These fine?"

"They're fine," Steph said, identifying Flynn's chosen utensil by the sound they had made.

He made quick work of the tape and lifted the flaps of the box. Content with the integrity of the shipped items, he picked the box up and headed for the back door.

Steph gave him a sideways look, "Where are you going?"

"I'm just going to set this up."

"And what about dinner?" Steph pointed her pen at the steamed bag sitting on the bench.

"It'll only take a minute," Flynn reassured, "besides you're kind of hogging the table right now."

"Shut up and go set up your stupid light," Steph said, pretending to be annoyed but unable to hide a smile. "I'll get things sorted in here."

He walked over to the table and gave her a kiss. "You're the best."

"Nah you," Steph said, her face now broken into a proper smile.

He kissed her again before leaving.

Flynn slid the back door half open and was greeted by a large German Shepherd. Solomon. Sol for short.

"Hey Sol," he said, ruffling the creature's ears. He called back into the kitchen, "Steph!"

"Yeah?"

"You fed Sol?"

"Thanks for volunteering. Food's in the back fridge."

"Alright." Flynn stepped outside, gently pushing Sol aside with his knee. "Let's get you fed m'boy. Just gimme a sec."

Another red brick path led Flynn to a small building half hidden by a stand of bamboo. Sol let out a small whine.

"Just give me a minute!" Flynn said while slipping inside. Sol settled outside the door with crossed paws.

The flat was relatively small but the space was well utilized. Five terrariums of varying sizes were placed against the walls, providing accommodation for any residents lucky enough to secure a booking in such a fine establishment as Flynn's back flat office. The population fluctuated anywhere from one to seven residents, all spread across the five terrariums and a single cluttered desk.

Steph had no aversion to his passion for arachnids but she did have a few guidelines. Keeping live specimens in the main house area was forbidden. Doubly so if they were venomous. And so

Flynn had set up a workspace where spiders – dead or alive – were allowed.

He set the package down on the aforementioned desk before peering into the closest terrarium, its interior resembling the Amazon.

It took a good minute of searching through the jungle he had created until he eventually found the flat's newest residents. Penelope and Camilla, a pair of Pinktoe Tarantulas indigenous to the real Amazon, and so called for the fuzzy pink tips at the end of each of their legs. The two spiders were cuddled up together under a heat lamp – unmoving – living up to their species' docile and gregarious reputation.

Having located the pair, Flynn grabbed the box off the desk and removed a new heat lamp. Sliding his hand behind Penelope and Camilla's terrarium, he plugged the cord in. He positioned the new lamp carefully inside the terrarium in the opposite corner to the two spiders. It would hopefully provide them with more warmth and humidity in their artificial jungle.

As foreigners, Penelope and Camilla had only arrived in Australia with careful planning. Getting one of them into the country had been difficult. The second? Near impossible. Countless emails and phone calls to customs, an arachnologist friend in the US, and a range of other colleagues had secured the appropriate permissions, paperwork and favours, eventually getting the girls safely over.

But his pink slippered ladies would hopefully have a companion soon. Deciding to run the gauntlet again, Flynn was in the process of securing them a breeding partner. He had just sent off the first email concerning the impending immigration before leaving the lab today.

Sol whined outside.

The new heat lamp secured without incident, Flynn slid the

enclosure's lid back on and crossed to a small bar fridge. He would return and check on his other resident later. In the meantime, Sol required his attention. And then – his own stomach.

Flynn removed a roll of dog food from the fridge, a knife from the top of the fridge, and a chopping board from beside the fridge. He left the flat for the patio table. Sol followed him the moment he was outside, mouth open in anticipation.

"Bowl?" Flynn asked.

Sol trotted over to the back door and lifted his metal bowl up with a *clang*. He trotted back to Flynn's side, placing the bowl in his open hand.

"Good boy."

The wet food adequately squared, Flynn slid it into the bowl, topping it off with some dry biscuits he scooped out of a bag by the back door. Dinner prep complete, Flynn set the bowl down in sight of the kitchen table, where Steph could be seen preparing their own dinner.

Sol chomped away at his food and Flynn returned to the main house.

"You took your time," Steph said with false severity, placing a fork beside Flynn's seat at the table.

"A dog's got to eat," Flynn returned.

"How's the new lamp?" Steph asked, sitting opposite the place she had just set.

"Perfect," Flynn said, sitting down as well. A bottle of shiraz sat between them. He picked it up, asking, "Wine?"

"Please," Steph said, sliding her glass within Flynn's reach. He poured a generous glass, earning a remark from Steph, "Are you trying to get me drunk, Mr. Schilder?"

"That's Dr. Schilder to you, Mrs. Schilder."

"Whatever."

The pair laughed.

4

"So…"

It was late and Flynn and Steph were in bed. The nights were beginning to warm and the window was open. A gentle breeze stirred the curtains. Sol lay at the end of the bed, his head down and eyes drooping.

Flynn continued speaking, "Isaac said the house is a few hundred metres into the bush. Said that we should ask the old man in the green caravan where it is."

"The old man in the green caravan?"

"That's what he said."

"Sounds like the start of a bad movie," Steph put her head under the sheet and pretended to be a ghost, "HOOOOOOOOOO."

Flynn hit her with a loose cushion.

Having heard the *smack* of the cushion, Sol's head poked up into view. There was concern on his canine face. Both Flynn and Steph laughed at the comical expression. Content that neither of his masters were in danger, Sol put his head back down.

Steph settled back down, resting a hand against Flynn's chest, "Did you ask the caravan park if he was allowed to come?"

"Yup."

"And?"

"Yup," Flynn said again.

"It will be nice to have him along."
"Yeah, we'll just have to watch out for snakes."
"And spiders," Steph said gravely.
Flynn smacked her with another cushion.

5

Bzzt.

It was the next morning and Flynn was back in the lab, the phone against his ear.

Bzzt.

This call was a little more international than his last. He was following up an email he had received from a colleague in the US overnight. It was concerning Flynn's next Pinktoe importation. Apparently there were going to be some complications.

Bzzt.

As Flynn's work day was beginning, his colleague's would be finishing. He was hoping to catch him at the office before he left.

The call rang out to an answering service. Flynn terminated the call, not bothering to leave a message, choosing instead to draft up his reply in an email.

Less than a minute later, his phone rang and he snatched it up, "Hello, Flynn."

"Hi Flynn," the voice on the other end was thick and Southern, "Sorry I missed your call."

"Hey Drew, not a problem. I was about to reply to your email, but thought a call would be better."

Flynn looked up at the sound of the lab door opening. A man walked in, a paper coffee cup in one hand and a waxed paper bag in the other. The bag contained donuts; he knew that without looking. Ever since Matt had signed on to help Flynn for post-grad credit, he had eaten donuts every morning. Matt raised his coffee hand in a silent greeting.

"Yeah…" Drew paused. "Don't think we're going to be able to manage it this time around."

"You said as much in your email," Flynn said, choosing his own words, "but what exactly are we talking?"

"You've got females, yeah?"

"Yup."

"And you're after a male?"

"Correct."

"And that's where we have our problem."

Flynn was silent for a minute. He knew this was going to be an issue. He also knew Drew was a by-the-book kind of guy. Wiggle room didn't really exist but somehow Flynn had to find it.

Drew kept going, "I know you want to breed them, and I know you're probably the best possible person over there to do so but anyone I talk to doesn't want to send you a male. They're too worried about customs."

"Are you telling them I've already got females?"

"Um, yeah?" Drew said, as if it was an obvious fact.

"Have you tried not telling them?"

There was a pause.

"Drew?"

"I can't do that for you Flynn."

"Okay okay okay, I understand," Flynn said, "let's leave this for a bit and see what we can do, right?"

Drew sighed, "Sure thing."

"Sounds like you need to go home," Flynn said.

"You have no idea. I'll talk to you later."

"No worries mate, enjoy your evening."

"And you your morning… mate."

Flynn hung up and walked over to Sheila's enclosure. He dropped a few live crickets in before returning to his desk.

"Morning Matt."

In answer, Matt swivelled on his chair to face Flynn, coffee cup in hand, "Trouble in the US of A?"

"Mmm…" Flynn said, "You remember the Pinktoes I got?"

"The ones I still haven't seen?" Matt said with a not-so-subtle hint, "Yeah."

"Trying to get a third over. A male."

"Oh?" Matt said with a raise of his bushy eyebrows. He took a sip of coffee. "Penelope and Camilla going to get a little freaky, are they?"

"Perhaps not…"

Matt's eyebrows crinkled into a quizzical mess, "Because…?"

"Suppliers are afraid of customs," Flynn said, "I guess they don't want to send one over and have it die if it gets detained."

"How do they even know you've got females?"

Flynn let some of his frustration show, "Drew doesn't believe in withholding any form of information."

"Bummer," Matt took another sip, eyes attracted to the dissection pad Flynn had covered over last night. "What you got under there?"

Flynn was glad for the change of topic. "You remember those emails I was getting from that teenager?"

"The kid who thought he'd discovered a new species?"

Flynn was silent and Matt lowered his cup.

"Serious?"

"He brought me a specimen yesterday afternoon. It was pretty beat up, but…" he couldn't keep the excitement out of his voice, "it's like nothing else."

"Got pics?"

"One second." Flynn woke his laptop with a jiggle and tapped out a password. He already had the photos open on the screen.

Matt leaned over his shoulder and scrolled through the images. Flynn began to rattle off a list of unique characteristics.

"Separated head and thorax. Unique colouration. Mouth on the underside. No evidence of pedipalps. Guessing a rough classification as a tarantula but," he exhaled, "it's like nothing else."

Matt let out a low whistle, echoing Flynn's statement, "Like nothing else. Where did he find it?"

Flynn didn't bother answering, accessing the flash drive Isaac had brought him and showing the videos of the boys investigating the old house and shed.

"Where's this taken?"

"Up Katoomba way."

"In the mountains?"

"Yeah. In some bushland. Pretty remote."

"No wonder the place is abandoned. Who would want to live up there?" Matt said, his love for city comforts bleeding through as he fondled his smartphone and paper coffee cup. "You going to go check it out?"

"Steph's picking me up this afternoon and we're headed up."

"And Sol?"

"He's coming with us."

"Aw man," Matt said, "I was hoping that mutt and I would finally get some time together again. You know my standing offer for when you guys are away."

"I know, I know," Flynn said, "but the park's going to let him in."

"Fair enough," Matt drained the rest of his coffee before tossing the cup into a bin across the room.

"Nice shot," Flynn remarked.

"I've been practising."

"Of course you have."

6

"You sure we took the right turn off?"

"The sign said Katoomba, why wouldn't I be sure?"

"Could be the fact that the road is now dirt."

"This is a shortcut." Steph gripped the wheel as they bounced along the dusty road.

Flynn gave her a sceptical look from the passenger's seat, "Not according to the GPS."

He flicked a switch on the side of the device, unmuting the voice of an automated British woman. "Turn back. Turn back. Turn back."

"She wants you to turn back," Flynn said.

Steph kept her eyes fixed angrily on the road.

Flynn looked out the window. It was dusk, and the sun had tucked itself behind the peaks of the Blue Mountains, their characteristic blue haze having deepened to navy in the dying sunlight. The headlamps of two rock climbers glimmered near the top of a far off cliff, the sheer face below them telling of their daylong conquest.

He turned his thoughts to what the weekend might hold. He had spent most of the car trip obsessing over possibilities. He had been temporarily distracted while navigating their way out of the city and afternoon traffic, a task that required complete concentration. But now – sitting in the passenger seat while his wife drove and Sol slept in the back – his thoughts and feelings were bubbling over.

He was on his way towards discovering a new species. He was sure of it.

Discovering a new spider was news worthy. It would blow up on social media. The university would beam with more pride than necessary. Other arachnologists would applaud him. It might even help him get his third Pinktoe into the country. Who could deny a world renowned arachnologist? It might even get the university to grease a few cogs and get him some more grant money to continue the studies he and Matt were currently doing. Such a grant would come at an opportune time. Most of their funding had dried up over the past few months.

But beyond the admiration, respect, and potential grants he would gain a new level of self-satisfaction in his work. His passion. The thrill of that would be enough.

"Ha!" Steph exclaimed, pulling off the dusty road and onto a highway, "Told you!"

Flynn stared out the window at the distant climbers who had now reached the top of their cliff, and said with a faint smile, "Well that's a relief."

7

Half an hour later they were walking along a small trail through the bush not far from their cabin. The sun had set and only traces of light reflected off the clouds. Now that they were in the mountains, a chill was creeping into the twilit air. They had dressed accordingly, wrapped in woollen sweaters.

The path through the trees was wide enough for Flynn and Steph to walk side-by-side. They both held torches, their beams playing against the surrounding eucalypts. Sol was ahead of them, straining against the lead in Flynn's hand, eager to frolic after being subjected to the confines of the car.

"Easy boy, we don't want you disappearing into the dark." Flynn tugged on the lead but it had no effect on Sol's enthusiasm.

"Did we really have to try to find it tonight?" Steph hugged herself.

"I just want to see if we can." Flynn didn't relish the idea of trying to get information from the old man. Isaac's description had been less than encouraging. "Besides, Sol's been cooped up in the car all afternoon and he didn't complain once," Flynn said. "He deserves it."

"Nice reason, but I'm cold and you've got all of tomorrow – and a crazy old man – to help you find it." Steph stopped. "We're heading back."

Flynn swept his torch beam around the dark bush. It reflected off the ghostly gums surrounding them. The house didn't reveal itself.

Sol still strained at the leash, unappreciative of the interruption. The man and his animal exchanged a look of shared unwillingness. Flynn then looked at his wife.

"Don't," she raised a cautionary finger, "don't you boys do this. You can come out here and wander until you go mad tomorrow. I'm not going to do it with you." She rubbed her arms. "Not in this cold."

"Fine," Flynn said, walking back towards his wife.

Sol let out a whine.

"Don't!" Steph said, glaring at the dog.

Sol lowered his head and trotted reluctantly back to the cabin behind them.

8

The sun had broken the mountaintops hours earlier, and sunlight filtered through the trees. Kids were racing around on bikes and scooters as Flynn retraced his steps from the night before to the rear of the caravan park, Sol keeping stride beside him.

Flynn had overcome his trepidation and was on his way to meet with the old man. Even if he was crazy, he might be able to save him hours of searching the bush himself.

It was closing on ten o'clock. He would have preferred an earlier start but Steph had advised him to avoid the possibility of coming across antagonistic by waking an old man earlier on a weekend. Flynn had pointed out that it likely didn't matter what day it was to a retired old kook living in a caravan park but she had been adamant. He had only been able to leave when ten o'clock had ticked closer and Steph could stand him hanging around no longer.

He had left her back at the cabin with her pile of marking, a promise of returning for lunch, and a kiss.

Reaching the rearmost limits of the park, Flynn discovered the caravan just as Isaac had described. It had suffered years of neglect, and its green siding had been badly stained with the brown of dirt and falling bark. A canvas room sagged beside the caravan, its most stable aspect being the doorframe erected in its side. The poor state of the setup had rendered it well camouflaged as they had passed into the bush last night.

Eager to get things over with, Flynn walked up to the door and rattled the fly-screen, shouting out with a smile, "Hello? Anyone there?"

Flynn heard a crash in response and a string of badly enunciated cuss words. Moments later, a door behind the fly-screened annex was opened. Flynn couldn't make out the resident's features.

"Who are you?" The man's words came out gummy. Flynn bet he had no teeth.

The fly-screen was pushed outwards into Flynn and he stepped back.

The old man came into full view.

He was bald. Entirely. Both his head and his face had given up trying to grow hair through his voluminous wrinkles. His eyes, nostrils, and mouth were the only reprieve from them, and even they seemed lost amongst the creases. His mouth hung half open, sucking in breath. Flynn's assumption had been only half right: three teeth still protruded from his pink gums but they were yellow with decay.

The man didn't look angry, despite his tirade at Flynn's knocking, but he did look expectant. He repeated, "Who are you?"

"Who am I?" Flynn confirmed that was what he asked with a glance. "My name is Flynn-"

"And?"

"And I'm an arachnologist from a university in Sydney. I just want to ask you a few questions, if that's okay?"

The old man grabbed his chin and contemplated him with suspicion. "You're from a university?"

"Yes, I'm from a university," Flynn smiled.

"And you have questions?"

"Yes yes, just a few questions." This wasn't as unpleasant as Flynn had imagined but he still wanted to move quickly. He really only had one question: "Where is the house?"

The old man, who had up until now seemed beyond senile, gave Flynn a knowing smile. "Ah, I see." Amusement gave way to panic. "You can't."

"Can't what?" Flynn played dumb.

"It's too close, too close." The senility resurfaced and he gave away the very information he was trying to withhold as he pointed into the bush. "It's too close to here. They'll get you."

"Who are they?"

The old man laughed, air making a whistling sound as it passed through his toothless grin. "You know who they are."

"Sir... what are you afraid of?"

The old man stiffened. He tried to stammer something out. Then he slammed his door shut and resumed his abuse of his broken dishes.

Flynn gave Sol a look and shrugged.

The pair ploughed into the bush, heading the direction the old man had pointed out.

It only took five minutes of walking before the two-storey house swung into sad sight.

It sat squat and sprawling amongst the encroaching bush. Its tin roofs had been eaten by moisture. Sunlight pierced through the rusted holes, illuminating greyed decking below wide verandahs. The house's windows were chasms of darkness. At least they still had glass in them.

But Flynn wasn't interested in the house.

Isaac had had spoken about a shed that was behind it. For the briefest moment Flynn considered walking through the derelict shell, effectively taking a shortcut, but walked around the house perimeter instead. Sol, upon seeing the house, had set off on his own path of exploration, and Flynn left him to his own devices.

Just as Isaac had said, the shed was hidden by an overgrown garden. Flynn pushed through the knee-high overgrowth until he reached it.

The swinging metal doors were chained shut, a detail Isaac had failed to mention.

Ever the optimist, Flynn pushed the doors away from each other, seeing if it was possible for him to slip between the gap with the chain still intact.

No luck. Flynn was simply too big. Isaac's scrawniness had obviously been helpful here. Probably why he hadn't bothered to mention it.

Flynn circled the overgrown shed, seeking out an alternative entry point. If he had known this was going to be a problem, he would have brought some bolt cutters. He felt a pang of guilt for a second but the place was abandoned. Nobody would care if a rusted chain was cut. He would have to see if the park manager had some bolt cutters he could borrow.

Unable to enter the shed but with a plan to do so later, Flynn turned his attention to the house.

He had equal hope and expectation that the spiders would be in the house as well. Isaac had told him the tunnel he had found ran under the house, although it narrowed to the point of being impassable, the teen had said. Hopefully he could still fit through.

Flynn pulled a small, cylindrical device out of his pocket. Spiders weren't particularly fond of having bright white light shone in their faces, so he had brought along a black light which simulated darkness for any eight legged friends he might find inside.

He rolled the torch between his hands and ascended to the porch.

Sol rejoined him. Flynn reached down and ruffled the animal's ears.

"You ready boy?"

Sol barked once in reply.

"Alright." There were butterflies in his stomach. "Let's see what we can find."

He pushed the door open and Sol plunged inside ahead of him. Without stepping over the threshold, Flynn looked in.

An ascending flight of stairs was visible, leading to a railed landing above. On the bottom floor, a central hallway ran from the front to the back of the house. Tall, narrow doorframes granted passage to various, invisible rooms on both the left and the right, dividing the house up into neat little boxes. A door nearly identical to the one he had just opened could be dimly seen at the front of the house.

Flynn stepped inside and thumbed the button on his torch. Black-purple light sprang forth to splash itself across the walls, revealing hidden stains. He scraped the beam around the cracks, corners, and crevices of the front entrance, pouring the light anywhere he thought a spider might hide.

Satisfied that the rear entrance held none of the sought arachnids, he moved into an old sitting room still filled with plastic-draped furniture.

The room had a slight scent of ash which emanated from the stained black of an old fireplace. Disregarding his clothing, Flynn climbed into it and scoured the chimney with his light. He would change later. Right now, he was trying to find spiders, and spiders loved abandoned dark places like nobody's business.

The sight of a few cobwebs sent his pulse racing until common sense kicked in. The spider he was looked for couldn't spin webs. The specimen he had examined lacked the required spinnerets. He wasn't looking for a catcher; he was looking for a hunter.

Webs weren't important.

He pulled his head out of the chimney and searched the rest of the room with no success. He left this room for another.

A dining table and chairs, coated in dust, sat in the middle of the room. Sol was in here, his nose sniffing the skirting boards, no doubt having caught scent of a residential rodent in the walls. Flynn had got to his training late, so Sol was useless at sniffing out spiders. Flynn wondered if that was even a thing.

Getting down on his hands and knees, Flynn checked under the table and chairs for any hiding arachnids. Finding none, he dusted himself off and walked across the hall and through the door leading to the kitchen.

An old wooden dining table sat against the wall, crammed between a decrepit fridge and cast iron wood stove. He crossed the creaking floor and scoured the purple light through the gaps behind the fridge and stove.

Nothing. Only a frayed electrical wire and long dead cock-roaches.

He continued his search, pulling on the handle of a nearby cupboard. The door came with the handle as he wrenched it off its rusted hinge, revealing nothing but swollen fibreboard shelves. He banged his way through the rest of the kitchen's cupboards and drawers, checking behind various collections of yellowing crockery and rusted utensils but with no success.

He stood in the middle of the room, considering his next move.

Sol trotted into the kitchen, having given up on finding any mice-sized play mates. He looked at his master with his head cocked, as if to ask: where next?

In answer, there was a bang above them. A second bang fol-lowed the first.

Sol let out a low growl and left the kitchen. Flynn followed and the pair headed for the stairs. Ascending, they arrived on the second floor.

A scent on his nose, Sol zeroed in on a closed door at the end of the upstairs hall. He pawed at it before looking at Flynn expectantly.

Flynn knew that look. It was Sol's *I-want-to-go-outside* look.

He drew closer to the door and stopped to listen.

Caw.

The hinges creaked as he pushed the door open. The room beyond was small and drab. Its lone window was missing its glass, letting a slight draft in from the bush outside. Lying in the middle of the room was a black mess of feathers.

Caw.

The source of the sound was a crow. The bird was lying on its side, its bony black legs scrabbling against the floorboards in a useless attempt to right itself.

Sol began to rush forward but Flynn grabbed his collar and commanded, "Stay." The German Shepherd obeyed and sat back on his haunches to watch.

Flynn knelt beside the struggling bird, agitating it with his proximity. But – despite its squawking, flapping, and scrabbling – it was unable to move more than a foot from its spot on the floor.

Its struggling grew weaker, until all it could do was look at Flynn with its one visible, beady, terrified eye. He reached out a hand and brushed its feathers just in time to feel its breathing come to a ragged halt.

9

"So," Steph said between mouthfuls, "what are you going to do now that the park owner thinks you're a bike thief?"

Flynn didn't reply, his own mouth filled with half-chewed food.

They sat in a small café. Sol was tied to a wooden telephone pole outside. The early afternoon sun fired through a large open window, the greasy smear of a small child's hand visible on the otherwise clean glass.

Flynn had returned to the cabin at midday to change, pick Steph up, and take her into town for lunch. On the trip in, he recounted the morning's fruitless search of the old house which had ultimately led to him attempting to borrow a set of bolt cutters from the park owner. Thanks to a few verbal blunders and ill-received jokes, his request had been denied and the owner's suspicions aroused. They were now discussing his plan going forward.

The mouthful finished, Flynn spoke, "Trying to figure that out now."

"More searching?"

Flynn had already shovelled more food into his mouth so he replied with a shrug. Once he was done he added, "And go buy some bolt cutters of our own I guess. Will head back this afternoon."

"So, you're going to leave me alone for even longer on our magical weekend away?"

"Not alone," Flynn returned, "you've got a whole bunch of papers to keep you company."

"Don't remind me," Steph said. "Although, there have been some good ones this morning."

"Distinction worthy?"

"One of them HD worthy."

"Well, that's some fun then."

Steph tried to snag a salad leaf, with little luck, "Want to check the town out this afternoon?"

"Um," Flynn chose his words, "I was going to go back to the house and-"

"Let me stop you for a second," Her voice lost its playful edge and she transformed into a lecturer, "You've searched the house top to bottom, correct?"

"Yes ma'am."

"And not a single, eight-legged, furry freak has shown even a tippy toe during?"

"Also correct."

"And you think these things are nocturnal?"

Flynn gave her a look, "How do you know that?"

"I've been married to an arachnologist long enough now to know certain things about certain types of spider," she shuddered a little bit, "and Isaac found it in pretty much the darkest place you can think of: underground?"

"Yup," Flynn was smiling now.

So was Steph. "So, I think that you think it's nocturnal which means..."

"I should check the place out tonight instead of this after-noon."

"More precisely, it won't matter if you check it out this afternoon," Steph finally snagged the lettuce, "or tonight."

"Okay… Well what are we going to do between now and then?"

"You are aware that this place is known for its tourism right?"

"Not really," Flynn said. "I came here for the spiders."

"Freak."

10

Flynn adjusted the strap of the bag slung across his back, its contents shifting around as he walked further into the bush, Sol in tow. Steph had insisted Sol accompany him again and had returned to her papers just as the sun started to set.

The bush was caught in dusky shadows. Bats flitted amongst the white eucalypts, their black wings beating the air as they twisted back and forth in pursuit of insects. Birds were making their final calls for the day before leaving the bush to the night shift. Far off Flynn could hear the beating thumps and crunches of kangaroos and wallabies traversing the undergrowth.

He shifted the bag again, this time slipping the second strap over his other shoulder to more effectively distribute its weight. Inside were the bolt cutters, various torches and batteries, a trio of durable specimen containers, and some snacks Steph had packed: chocolate bars for Flynn and jerky for Sol. She made sure she took care of her boys. Dinner would be waiting for them all upon the pair's return.

The trek to the abandoned house seemed shorter this time, their route the more sure after the previous visit.

Keen to explore unvisited spaces first, Flynn walked around the edge of the house to the shed. Having already investigated the surrounding area this morning, Sol dutifully accompanied him.

Flynn let the bag slide off his shoulders to the ground. He knelt, rummaging around inside for the compact set of bolt cutters he had bought in town. His hand snagged a torch in the process, and he slipped it into a pocket beside his black light. His other hand pulled out the cutters.

He pinched the hardened metal loop of the padlock between the edges of the bolt cutters. Bearing down on the plastic wrapped handles, he snipped the padlock open without difficulty. Unlooping the chain from the now broken lock, he let the shed door creak wide.

In the shadows of dusk, the air turned entirely black only a metre in. Flynn was hit with the stench of rotted straw and musty wood. Cool, damp air reached out from the dark, beckoning the pair.

Sol darted inside.

Lifting the bag back to a single shoulder, Flynn stepped past the threshold and into the dark.

He let his eyes adjust until he could see nothing but an empty space. He could barely make out Sol sniffing around the murky edges.

"Sol!" Flynn said, louder than he meant, "Come!"

The animal followed the instruction. Flynn didn't want him to be a disruption in his searching. If the spiders would be found anywhere, it would be in the corners where he was shoving his nose. He also recalled Steph's warning, Make sure he doesn't get bitten. While the spiders he was looking for didn't have fangs, others did, and they were in prime Funnel Web territory.

Flynn thumbed on his black light and lightly stepped to the edges of the shed. Sol, still heeding his master, hung back.

Just as his nose had confirmed, the thick wooden beams forming the shed's floor were strewn with black spotted straw.

As Flynn shuffled through the detritus, stray strands of straw fell through the cracks to the cellar below.

Isaac had mentioned the trap door that led downwards and Flynn now looked for the tell-tale rope that would open it.

As if detecting Flynn's objective, Sol walked over and sat on top of a board of wood, the rope snaking out beneath his paws.

"Good boy," Flynn affirmed, gently pushing Sol off.

Flynn tugged the rope up and the trap door slammed down hard, causing Sol to bark in fright.

"Shh Sol. Nothing to be worried about."

Regarding the now open trap door suspiciously, Sol made the decision regarding worry himself. Content, he plunged down the steps before Flynn could say anything.

Not wanting Sol to disturb any exposed spiders, Flynn quickly descended behind, scolding the dog, "Sol! Come back here!"

On the way down, Flynn banged his head on the low lying roof, momentarily distracting himself from his reprimanding.

"Ouch," he muttered, his shoulders now hunched in the low space.

A concerned muzzle poked his hand out of the darkness.

Flynn caught Sol in purple light. The animal's ears were drooped and his tail limp, his eyes looking up in apology.

"It's alright boy, nothing I can't handle," Flynn assured him, ruffling his ears until they perked back up. "Now, let's have a look around down here."

Walking about with bent knees, Flynn investigated the space.

Except for a stagnant pool of water in one corner and bits of straw, the cellar was empty.

It had been carved out of a solid bed of sandstone, the wooden beams above laid across an excavated hole. The space had been created for function, so whoever had dug it out hadn't bothered to smooth the rough stone walls. Flynn swept his light through the various cracks and nooks that pocked them, but there wasn't even a tell-tale leg to be seen. Not even poking out from behind the lone set of shelves down here.

Flynn looked up, seeing the etched symbols Isaac had described. There were thousands of them, each a variation of the one beside it. All of them were greyed with age. Some had faded to near imperceptibility, even under the revealing purple of the torch.

Sol barked, causing Flynn to jump and drop the torch.

"Sol! What on earth is going-" Flynn stopped, seeing what Sol had barked at.

The dropped torch was pointing in the opposite direction of Flynn's line of vision, its light all but useless on the floor. And yet, a comparable purple light was shining at the opposite end of the cellar in a floor-to-ceiling crack.

Just to be sure it wasn't a trick of pre-existing light, Flynn scooped up the torch and clicked it off.

The crack of purple light remained.

Pocketing the torch, Flynn moved to investigate. Sol moved out of his way as he felt along the stone wall, his hand disappearing into a crack that would have remained hidden if it wasn't for the light.

Isaac hadn't mentioned this.

He continued to feel up and down the crack, determining its width and depth. He tried to peer in but the purple light hung on the air in a haze, making it impossible to see anything beyond it.

Setting his bag down beside the crack, Flynn stripped off his jacket and shoved it inside.

Sol pawed at his leg, anxious.

"It's okay boy," Flynn said, "I'm just going to see if I can fit through." The animal didn't seem comforted so he added, "If I can fit, you'll be able to fit too."

And with that, Flynn pushed a shoulder into the crack. The rough stone brushed against him as he moved through the crack sideways. It widened the further he moved in, until he could walk down the crack as if it was a hallway to some room waiting beyond.

Flynn stopped and called back to Sol in an encouraging voice, "Come on boy! You can come too."

Seconds later, Sol appeared behind him. Worry still hung about the animal as he sniffed the air.

"It's alright Sol." Flynn considered the possibility of dogs suffering from claustrophobia. "It's just a cave."

Still unsure, but ready to trust his master, Sol followed behind Flynn as they pressed deeper into the crack.

It eventually spilled out into an old mine. Rusted rails were embedded in the ground and wooden frames pressed up, preventing the earth from crashing down on top of them.

The purple light surrounded them as if it was coming from the air instead of a more conventional source.

Flynn looked around for any signs of arachnid activity but was distracted by the discovery of the mine and its odd, purple light. Should he find any spiders, it would only be a short trip back to his bag and a specimen container.

Rethinking his last thought, Flynn quickly squeezed back through the crack and retrieved a container and his jacket. Who knew how deep the mine was. A 'short' trip back might turn out longer than anticipated. Sure, carrying the container in one hand might prove awkward but he wouldn't forgive himself if he left to get a container only to find the spider had disappeared. It wasn't like Sol could keep an eye on it while he was gone.

Sol had shadowed Flynn back through the crack and pushed against his legs, wanting to get back into the cellar.

"Sol!" Flynn found himself reassuring the animal again, "It's alright."

Flynn considered something else. As far as Steph knew, he was checking out an old house, a shed, and a cellar. Not a mine. And the purple light, which had been the only thing that had drawn his attention to the otherwise hidden crack, might not be a permanent phenomenon.

If something were to happen, he would simply disappear.

He stepped out of the crack and into the cellar.

Sol shot past him to the other side of the subterranean room, content to put as much distance as possible between himself and the glowing crack.

Flynn ignored the animal, ascended the short steps, and exited the shed. The last rays of sun were disappearing from the upper foliage of the surrounding eucalypts as the bush gave itself fully to the night.

Flynn pulled his phone from a pocket and sent Steph a message.

With his wife informed, he turned back to the shed and descended into the cellar.

Sol was still pressed against the far wall, his eyes fixed on the purple crack.

"Come on boy," Flynn said, confidently striding back to the crack and inserting a shoulder, "let's go explore."

Not without hesitancy, Sol dutifully followed his master into the underground world beyond the purple glow.

11

Steph's phone buzzed on the laminated table top she was using as a workspace. The buzz was singular and long. A message.

Mired in the nightmarish prose of a first year student, filled with adverbial statements and sweeping generalisations, she didn't check the device. Instead, her pen continued to slash red across the page for the next fifteen minutes. In that time, she had mercifully put down the essay, resulting in a grade that could only be considered good if one were to operate under the mantra of 'Ps equal Degrees'. She had held back on a full evisceration of the student's literary aspirations but not without great restraint.

She flipped her phone over to a message from Flynn.

Found a crack in the cellar that leads into an old mine. There's some weird purple light coming out of it... Going to check it out. Have left my bag beside it just in case the light disappears. Sol is coming with me, seems a bit spooked though.

Contemplating a reply that wasn't too steeped in wifely admonitions and warnings, she settled on: *What about the spiders? Be safe.*

Knowing her husband, Flynn was already down in the mine. It was a miracle he had even thought to let her know what he was doing. A smart move but one he wouldn't normally contemplate. He was impulsive and excitable by nature which sometimes meant he forgot things.

She briefly considered going out there and accompanying him, just to be safe, but she quickly scolded herself for having such a motherly thought. He knew what he was doing and – besides – she had sent Sol along with him.

She could understand the dog's hesitancy at entering the mine. He had never been a fan of close spaces. He had never slept in a kennel, not even when they had kept him outside when allergic family were visiting. He preferred his outside to feel like he was outside. She could understand that. In fact, she didn't like caves herself, which gave her further justification to keep herself where she was and leave the boys alone.

With a small sigh, she lifted the pen once again and shifted another essay off the 'to do' pile to the space in front of her. This one was hideously entitled: "The Promethean Creation of Frankenstein and its Modern Relevance to an Analysis of Anthropological Philosophy".

Gag.

12

Flynn and Sol had reached their third junction inside the mine.

The purple light was disorienting, so Flynn had taken measures to prevent them getting lost. His jacket had been deposited at the entrance of the crack and a chocolate bar marked every corner they turned. He had considered using Sol's jerky as markers, but the chances of him eating their way back to the outside world were too high.

Sol had been hanging behind Flynn ever since they had entered the cave. His spirit of adventure seemed sapped by the purple air and stone passages.

With the air already glowing, both torches remained in Flynn's pocket as they sought the source of the light. If there was one.

As was often the case with mines, the passages all slanted downwards, taking them deeper into the earth and whatever minerals had once been at the end of the network. If he recalled correctly, Katoomba had once had a robust coal and shale mining industry. He had the afternoon's wanderings to thank for that little fact.

The passage suddenly spilled out into a huge cavern that would easily hold their entire home inside it. Close ceilings gave way to a soaring, cathedral-like height ascending into darkness.

In here the purple light was far less concentrated perhaps due to its monolithic size. It intensified again on the other side of the cavern, pouring out of another crack.

A collection of barely visible lumps lay in the middle of the cavern.

Encouraged by the more open space and a lessening of the purple light, Sol ventured in front of Flynn towards the lumps. His nose twitched as he sniffed.

And then Flynn could smell it too. Festering decay.

He joined Sol near the largest lump. The smell grew stronger. He withdrew one of the torches and clicked it on.

They were dead kangaroos. Bones protruded out of decaying flesh and matted fur.

Flynn pointed the torch up, trying to see the ceiling but with no luck. There must be some sort of hole in the roof the un-fortunate animals had fallen through but he couldn't confirm it without more powerful lighting.

Some of the animals had tried to move after landing down here but had only managed to drag themselves a short distance before life left them. Dark stains trailed behind these independent lumps to the larger pile of dead animals.

Flynn shuddered and lifted a hand to his nose. Sol was still sniffing, moving closer to the pile.

"Come on boy," Flynn said, "you don't need to touch that."

Sol moved back towards the tunnel that had brought them here.

"No boy, this way," Flynn said, pointing at the glowing tunnel on the other side of the cavern.

Sol barked in protest.

"I'm not leaving you alone down here. Come."

Another bark.

"Sol…" Flynn warned, "Come."

Sol whimpered.

"Hey," Flynn crossed over to him and knelt. "Hey." He lifted Sol's head and looked him in the eyes while ruffling his ears. "It's okay. Come on."

Reassured, but not convinced, Sol kept whimpering.

"It won't be much longer, promise." He pushed the animal's head against his chest.

After a few minutes buried in Flynn's arms, Sol stopped whimpering.

"Promise," Flynn said again, releasing Sol from the hug, "now come on."

They crossed the cavern, skirting around the rotten piles of kangaroo.

The glowing fissure yawned open. It was rough and natural looking. The ground was no longer level and smooth. The mine seemed to stop with the cavern they were leaving but this crack remained almost as wide as the man-made tunnels they had been traversing.

Flynn pushed forward.

Almost immediately upon entering the natural cave system, the light grew stronger. It had been intensifying the deeper they travelled but now it reached a level that began to sting Flynn's eyes, causing him to squint. They must be getting closer to its source.

Up until now, Flynn hadn't thought once about spiders, despite the container he still held in his hand. He briefly considered turning back. After all, he was here to find spiders not to mount a caving expedition.

But he couldn't shake his curiosity. Abandon a cave? Sure. But the purple light? Arachnologists suffered from rampant curiosity just as much as any other scientist. If you talked to Steph, Flynn was chronic. It didn't matter the phenomenon or subject. If one spider had been found, others would be found too. As for this light… Flynn had never seen anything like it. He had never even heard of anything like it.

The only other thing that gave him pause was Sol. He was a big dog and small spaces were far from his favourite kinds of places but he was behaving oddly. He had never been as stubborn as he was being now. Something had him spooked. Ever since they had entered, he'd hung behind Flynn. Normally, Flynn was lucky to be two steps behind the animal.

If he didn't find the light source soon, he would turn back for Sol's sake.

Having only gone less than ten metres into the new tunnel, Flynn found himself back in the mine. Rails on the ground and A-frames keeping everything held up.

He recalled a cave-in at an earlier junction which had forced him along the path that had brought him here. This must be the part of the mine it had cut off. Some stroke of naturally born luck had provided him a path back to it.

He pulled a chocolate bar from his pocket, placed it on the left side of the tunnel's exit and proceeded in the new direction, his decision made on a whim.

The light's intensity increased with every step. They must be close. On cue with the thought, they found themselves at a dead end.

But only in a horizontal sense. A rusted ladder poked up out of a vertical shaft. A purple spotlight blazed on the roof above it, the light pouring out of the hole in the ground.

Flynn had found his source.

With slitted eyes, he tried to look down, but the ladder quickly disappeared into a haze of purple light.

He looked into Sol's eyes, which glowed purple like every-thing around them. "Looks like this is the end of the line for you boy. Ladders aren't designed for dogs."

Flynn put a single foot on the first rung and pressed down. It held. He stomped on it twice just to be sure, and it remained sturdy.

He began his descent. Just as his head was about to enter the hole, Sol whimpered. He stopped.

"Hey boy," Flynn's voice was soothing, "it's okay. I won't be gone long. Promise."

Sol moved closer and licked Flynn's face before resting his head on his shoulder. Flynn reached up with a single hand and ruffled his ears, "I'll be right back."

Flynn descended.

He reached the bottom without incident and brushed his hands off on his pants. Steph wouldn't be happy with the rust stains they left. Some more pants to add to the weekend work drawer.

The light was blinding down here. He tried to shield his eyes but without effect. The light permeated the air.

Resorting to barely open eyes in an attempt to control the glare the light was now causing, Flynn saw its origin point.

A fissure from floor to ceiling, wide enough to fit his shoulders and nothing else, was only metres away from the bottom of the ladder.

Sol started to bark above him. He sounded so distant down here.

"It's alright Sol! I'm okay!" He shouted up.

Flynn moved for the crack, stepping carefully due to his limited vision.

Up until now he hadn't speculated on what could be causing the glowing purple light. The way it hung on the air, he suspected some sort of bioluminescent phenomenon was present. Airborne algae maybe? But the way it seemed to pour out of tunnels and cracks, and intensify, had led him further and further down here in search of a source that must exist.

Now he had found it. Speculation would give way to observation and he wasn't quite sure what to expect.

Exercising caution, he put his hand into the crack and felt around. The sides of the crack were smooth… almost glass-like.

Pushing deeper, his arm turned a corner. The crack wasn't deep at all. He was incapable of seeing whatever lay beyond but it was less than half a metre in.

Satisfied that he had taken the required amount of caution before squeezing himself into a confined space, Flynn pushed through the crack. He had to suck his stomach in a couple of times but in a matter of seconds he was through to the other side.

His eyes were still trying to adjust to the light but in here it seemed to lessen, enabling him to see the wondrous sight before him.

The cavern he now found himself in was coated in purple and white crystals, some large and some small, all of them causing light to shatter and sparkle in a thousand different ways as it ascended to a high, curved ceiling.

He was standing inside a massive geode.

At the base of the egg-shaped cavern was a pool of glowing liquid. Agitated by a subterranean current, it cast shifting patterns of purple light against the crystalline structure of the cave. A low thrumming sound faded in and out with the slow pulsing of the pool's light, causing the air to vibrate.

Incredible.

Carefully straddling giant chunks of crystal sprouting from the floor, Flynn worked his way to the edge of the pool. He tried to peer into it when the strength of the light was at the lowest end of the pulse but it was still blinding.

What on earth was this place?

Flynn circled the pool's circumference, his path clear of any obstructing crystal formations. The entire edge of the pool was translucent crystal. While the surface was smooth, the pulse of the pool's light lit up web-like cracks inside.

The edge, before crystal gave way to water, was encircled with strange runes. He knelt and traced his finger through the grooves of one. Its entire form flowed together without interruption, breaking only to progress to the rune beside it.

Having completed his circumnavigation of the pool, Flynn estimated that it was easily ten metres across, if not more. It was hard to tell. The all-pervading light did not make scientific measurement or estimation an easy task.

He turned his attention to the water itself, kneeling down on the circle of runes.

His gut a mix of excitement, dread, and the unknown, Flynn dipped a hand into the glowing water. A zap of warmth rocketed through his hand into the rest of his body. He yanked it out and stumbled back, holding his breath. A buzz lingered for a few seconds before fading. He let his breath out.

No permanent damage done. Except something was off…

He lifted the hand that had just been in the pool up in front of his face, examining it. To be sure, he felt it with his other hand.

It was completely dry. Not a single drop clung to his hand.

He dipped his hand back into the pool.

The warmth flooded him again. He held his hand there and stared into the blinding light of the pool, losing himself in it. His body pulsed with the fading in and out of the pool's light. He no longer heard the sound of the air. He felt it coming from inside him.

He closed his eyes.

When he opened them, he was no longer kneeling by the pool's edge. He was knee deep and fully clothed, slowly walking towards the centre of the pool through no conscious thought of his own. His body had begun to displace the liquid filling the pool, causing it to spill into the encircling runes. Where liquid met each rune, they had begun to glow brightly.

Panic bolted through Flynn and he quickly retreated beyond the smooth edge of the pool to the chunks of crystal that surrounded it.

The liquid eased out of the runes' grooves and ceased to glow.

What had just happened?

Somehow he had been hypnotized. Whether it was the pool, the light, the sound, or something else entirely, he didn't know. All he knew is that one second he had closed his eyes and the next he was in the pool.

He felt his pants. Just like his hands had been before, they were inexplicably dry.

Still beset with scientific curiosity, although now liberally mixed with fear of the unknown, Flynn approached the pool again.

With cupped hands, he scooped some of the liquid up and dumped it on top of a rune. For the brief few seconds that liquid filled it, the rune blazed with a light brighter than the pool's. As the liquid drained, the light faded.

He scooped up more water, repeating the process with the same result.

What would happen if all the runes were flooded at the same time? Flynn wondered.

The only way to do that would be to displace the water enough for the pool to cover all the runes at once. And to do that he would need…

He left the edge of the pool, searching around for anything he could throw into the water. Despite the myriad of crystal clusters that surrounded him, none of them were loose enough to dislodge.

For a brief second he debated simply walking into the pool far enough to displace the required amount of liquid. When he had been knee deep and only a couple of metres into the pool, the runes had already been half-filled. He would only need to go waist deep to fill the runes completely.

But he decided against it. He had no idea what could happen. Whatever was going on here, it broke the laws of physics, and that – unbelievably – meant anything could be possible.

An idea struck him. The cave in.

It was hundreds of metres back in the old mine but piles and piles of loose rocks had littered the mineshaft floor near it.

Flynn turned to leave, only then realising something important. In all the excitement and mystery, he hadn't taken note of the entry point into the geode. New panic seized him.

He didn't know how to get out.

13

Steph massaged her temples with two fingers, staring at the screen she had placed amongst the sea of papers. Unable to subject herself further to the torturous words of her students, she had settled on an alternative – but equally infuriating – task.

Coffee this late hadn't helped.

Earphones had come out with the laptop, providing her with some escape from her tedious data entry as she digitized the remarks and numbers she had assigned to her students. The classical music soothed her frustrations, carrying her along with its dancing strings, soaring wood wind, and booming percussion.

She checked her phone. It was not long past eight o'clock.

Steph unlocked the device to her conversation with Flynn. She had replied to his last message over two hours ago and he hadn't seen it yet.

Although reticent to give too much voice to the worry building inside her, she tapped out a simple message: *How are things going?* She locked the phone and placed it face up on the unmarked pile of papers, trying to put it out of her mind and focus on her work.

Seconds later the screen flashed bright, informing her that the message had failed to send. Worry started to gnaw.

What if he had gotten lost in the mine? What if he was trapped?

She shook the thoughts off as over imaginative products of irrational logic, much like many of the arguments she had just marked.

Part way on track again, she shuffled through the essays, looking for one she enjoyed. Finding the paper with "HD" and multiple exclamation marks in the upper right hand corner, she began to solidify her blow-by-blow remarks into an overall comment on the essay itself.

Only minutes after starting, Steph stopped. She tried to hear the outside world from beneath the music. She paused it, removing the wires from her ears and listening.

Any success she had previously had in quelling what she thought to be irrational fears evaporated.

She turned around, looking at the door to the cabin.

There was Sol – barking like a mad dog – and pacing back and forth outside the door.

Worry exploded into fright and she bolted to her feet, sending papers flying.

"Sol!" Steph slid the door open. "Where's Flynn?"

Unable to answer her question with words, Sol barked once and ran onto the road. He looked back at Steph expectantly.

"Where's Flynn?" Breathing suddenly hurt. Sol wouldn't leave Flynn alone. Not unless…

Steph grabbed a jacket and the keys to the cabin. It had turned pitch black outside save for the odd street lamp or camp fire, so she rummaged through a bag for a torch. She clicked it on and then off, confirming that it was in working order, before stepping outside.

Sol was pacing on the road, eyes fixed on Steph's. He barked again. She had never seen him this upset.

"Where is he Sol?" Steph asked, trying to keep the panic out of her voice. "Where's Flynn?"

In answer, Sol took off towards the back of the caravan park, heading in the direction he had taken with Flynn hours before-hand. She knew where he was heading. The house. The shed. Flynn.

They passed the green caravan whose occupant Flynn had visited this morning. No lights were on inside. The old man must be asleep already.

Sol trotted past the caravan without a glance, leading her straight into the looming blackness of the bush.

Steph took a breath and switched on the torch.

14

"Sol!" Flynn called out. He stopped to listen for any reply but none came.

His initial reaction to his predicament had been panic but it had only lasted a brief moment. Up until now, he had taken special care to document the path he had taken. All he had to do was find the right crack and ladder and he would be able to get out.

He was feeling his way around the walls of the geode, hands seeking the crack he had lost in all the excitement. He was already half way around the geode without any success but it only meant he was getting closer to finding the exit.

Everything was under control.

His concern was no longer for his own well-being but Sol's. Ever since realising that he had lost the way out, he had called out for him but hadn't received a reply.

What if he had wandered off into the mine and gotten lost? Would he be able to find his way out? He stood a better chance than Flynn but that didn't stop him worrying. He had been so cagey the entire time they had been down here and Flynn was concerned how that might manifest itself further.

The best thing he could do for Sol – and himself – was to find his way out of here.

Another thing he had taken note of since searching for the exit was the time. He had lost all sense of it since plunging into the mine. The discovery of the geode and its mysterious pool had exacerbated that even further. He had been gone for hours. Steph might be getting worried.

As much as he disliked the thought, he was going to have to return some other time, maybe even with one of his more geologically minded friends. This phenomenon was well beyond the field of arachnology and even the wider net of biology. Even then, he was committed to discovering any other insights, scientific field be damned.

No, he would return to the mine, conduct some cursory searches in various nooks and crannies for the spiders he had come for, and then return to Steph. Anything else would have to happen tomorrow or some other weekend. The house, shed, and mine weren't going anywhere.

His back turned to the pool, Flynn's mind started to wander back to spiders.

The weekend had been a failure, at least by the standards he had set out with. He hadn't seen a single spider that matched the specimen Isaac had delivered to him. He could continue exploring but the chances of finding anything living this deep in the mine were slim.

The entire geode went black without warning, the purple light sucked out of the air, leaving Flynn stumbling. He pinned his back against a hunk of crystal, its rough edges digging at his skin through his clothes.

Then – as suddenly as it had disappeared – the purple light flooded back. Except this time, it was different. It no longer pulsed, but blazed steadily. The runes were fully lit. The entire cavern was awash with a light so bright, it began to lose its purple hue.

A shifting mass of shadows began to rise out of the water, tainting the bright light. A torrent of crawling black poured up over the runes, blotting out even their light.

Flynn remained pinned against the wall, straining to make out any more details.

Whatever was coming up out of the pool was alive. A whole lot of alive.

Flynn didn't know what to expect. In this subterranean world of strange glowing pools and gigantic geodes, anything might be possible.

The rising black mass seemed sinister but when it finally broke the surface of the water and crawled over the crystal ring surrounding the pool, nothing malevolent lurched forward to suck the life from him.

No longer obscured by the glowing water, the black form became more distinct. Flynn could make out individual forms.

They were spiders. Thousands and thousands of spiders, pouring from every edge of the pool and into the cavern. With startling speed they scaled the crystal walls, some of them rushing around Flynn's feet in the process.

Careful not to crush any of the spiders still rushing to the walls, Flynn turned on the spot, taking in the sight with mouth agape.

The overwhelming sparkle of the cavern was now fractured by flitting obstructions as the shadowy forms of thousands of spiders crawled all over the crystal walls. At his current distance, he couldn't make out any details but excitement began to well up inside him.

Flynn walked over to the nearest wall, being careful not to trip on any of the crystal formations that threatened to catch his feet as his attention was held elsewhere. Pulling the black light from his pocket, he shone it on the spider-coated wall. He was greeted by a sight he had been searching all day for.

Isaac's specimen looked exactly like these spiders, except the creatures coating the geode walls were far larger than he had expected and all of them had their legs firmly attached. Long and slender, they swelled at the knee joint before tapering into wicked looking pointed feet. Their three segmented bodies writhed as they moved, their heads swivelling as they looked around with large unblinking eyes.

Flynn unsnapped the lid of the specimen container he had faithfully carried the entire way through the mine. It was barely big enough to fit one of the larger spiders so he hunted around for a small one. Finding one, he lowered the container over the spider, sliding the lid against the wall and captured the creature in a plastic prison.

At last, a live specimen!

He placed the container on a crystal outcrop not far from the wall and returned to observing the spiders as they clambered over each other.

His heart pulsing, Flynn found a patch of bare wall beside one of the spiders and placed his hand against it. The crystal was warm to the touch, charged with the same energy as the pool, but in a far milder voltage.

The spider sensed Flynn's nearby hand, regarding it with a cocked head, but didn't flinch. Curious, it shifted its body to fully face the hand. Still curious, perhaps sensing his human warmth, it placed its forward feet against the flesh of Flynn's hand. A sharp prickle almost startled Flynn as the feet shifted over his hand but he remained still as the spider continued to investigate this intrusion in its strange world.

It crawled up fully onto Flynn's hand, completely covering his hand, its legs extending as far as Flynn's fingers. The weight of the spider now hung off Flynn's skin.

Despite being an arachnologist, this sensation – the sensation of a spider against his skin – always made Flynn's insides crawl. Fear, dread, and excitement roiled inside him. Unlike other animals, spiders never indicated when they might attack. It was part of what made them such perfect predators. And fascinating scientific subjects.

With slow movements, Flynn pulled his hand off the wall, the spider still firmly latched on. He brought his face close and shone the black light onto the spider, keen to conduct a close examination of the living creature.

Flynn slowly twisted his hand around, confirming all of the features he had observed back at the lab. Separated head and thorax, calling into question its arachanid classification (he'd solve that issue later); large forward facing eyes that shone purple in the dim light of the pool; and a bulbous abdomen that was dusted with grey and purple hairs that also caught the light.

All of this he confirmed with a glance before shifting his attention to the creature's legs, a previously unbeheld part of its anatomy.

While it had sat on the wall, he had conducted an initial inspection of the spider's eight legs, but had not been able to fully explore why its knees were so swollen. The rest of the legs – including the first limb connecting said knees to the thorax – were spindly, like a Hunstman Spider's gangly legs that enabled it to dart onto its prey. But the knees were bulbous to the point of ridiculousness. Moving beyond the strange knee joints, the rest of each leg tapered down to a point. Each leg – save the dark grey knees – bristled with fine purple hair.

As Flynn had shifted his hand around, the spider had remained still. Now that his hand had stopped moving, the two of them stared at each other.

"You're beautiful," Flynn said, marvelling at his discovery.

Then – without warning – its eight swollen knees burst open, a hooked, hypodermic needle firing down from each one into Flynn's skin below. Blossoming fire erupted in Flynn's hand as the eight fangs delivered eight simultaneous doses of venom into his bloodstream. He tried to shake the spider off, but its fangs were still firmly buried in his flesh. It was latched on and wouldn't let go.

Frantic to release its hold, Flynn moved away from the wall, shaking his hand furiously.

Then the spider let go but not before Flynn stumbled backwards over a chunk of crystal embedded in the geode floor. His head met the ground with a sickening crack and everything went black.

15

The abandoned house loomed out of the darkness, its black windows leering at Steph. The sight caused her to stop. It didn't look sad as Flynn described. It looked evil.

She shook her head, clearing the thought away. Her students' bad writing and the gloom of Shelley's gothic masterpiece were effecting her.

Sol was paces ahead of her but had stopped when Steph had. He looked back expectantly and pawed the ground, indicating the direction they had to go.

Flynn had said the shed was behind the house and the old mine beneath the shed… somewhere. She was hoping Sol knew where they were headed, otherwise Flynn was likely toast.

She shook her head again. After all of this, she was going back to the cabin and reading a damn classic to scrub away the taint of unpractised writing she had been exposed to over the weekend.

Sol barked at her, anxious to keep moving.

"Alright, let's go," Steph said, setting off again.

Sol took off around the side of the house, disappearing from view.

Steph followed at a slower pace, shining her torch into the side windows of the house. The old, fogged windows diffused the white light. She could see nothing but dim shadows inside as she moved along the side of the house.

Sol swung into view, standing in the overgrown backyard waiting for Steph. He barked again before plunging into the yawning mouth of an overgrown shed.

Steph took a deep breath, trying to calm the lightness in her stomach. Old brown grass swished against her legs as she closed the distance to the shed.

Musty air hit her in the face the moment she entered. She swung her torch beam back and forth, finding Sol standing by an open trapdoor at the back.

He disappeared, his claws clicking against wooden steps.

She descended, stooping as she entered the low cellar space, her hand brushing against the symbol riddled beams holding up the shed floor. This was by far the oddest shed she had ever encountered. Who built a cellar in Australia? Except for wine.

Sol was sitting beside Flynn's backpack which was resting against the rough stone wall of the cellar. It was half unzipped. Classic Flynn.

And then Sol turned, disappearing into the wall of the cellar through a hidden crack. A few seconds after disappearing, his head reappeared.

Steph crossed to the crack and Flynn's bag. Kneeling, she rummaged around until she produced a small first aid kit she had insisted Flynn take along – just in case. Now she was grabbing it… just in case. She shoved it into her jacket pocket.

Patting Sol's head, she pushed him into the crack before entering herself. Moments later she was on the other side in the old mine Flynn had found.

She pointed the torch in either direction, the white light engulfed in the murky dark. "Alright boy, where is he?"

Sol took off to the left of the crack, leading her on the downward slope into the rest of the mine. Steph followed at a trot.

They soon reached a junction, the mine branching off in two opposite directions. Without hesitation, Sol headed to the right and Steph followed, but not before she squished a chocolate bar placed by the right corner.

She smiled. Her husband wasn't a complete idiot. It gave her some small comfort in this dark, unknown place.

Sol charged through three more similar junctions and past a cave in before they reached a large, rank smelling cavern that seemed more natural than man-made. Piles of kangaroo carcasses littered its floor, forcing Steph to pull her scarf up over her nose to block out the smell.

Sol had slowed, exhibiting hesitation for the first time since he had returned to the cabin.

Steph's throat caught and she dearly hoped the only thing she could smell was dead kangaroo. Her mind flashed with vivid imaginings. Her proximity to the animal corpses didn't help. But she shook it off. So had Sol, who was now on the other side of the cavern waiting for her.

She wove her way through the piles of dead kangaroo and followed him through another hidden crack, this one more restrictive than the one between the cellar and the mine.

After much wiggling, Steph made it through the restriction.

On the other side the walls closed in again. She was back in the mine.

She heard Sol whimper in the darkness to her left and she swung the torch to illuminate the animal.

He was staring down into a vertical shaft, a rust red ladder poking out the top.

Steph closed the distance between them and stared down the shaft, the beam of her torch reaching only so far before it disappeared into a murky grey that washed out any details.

"Flynn's down there?" She asked Sol, gesturing with the torch beam.

Sol barked once, placing a paw on the top of the ladder.

I guess that's a yes, Steph thought.

"Alright," she said to herself, taking a few deep breaths before repeating herself, "alright."

Sol moved his paw as she lowered herself onto the ladder. Satisfied it would hold her weight – for crying out loud it held Flynn's – she started climbing down.

Just before her head disappeared into the hole, Sol whimpered and licked her face.

Under normal circumstances, such an act earned a quick scolding. But he was scared, and so was she.

"I'll be right back, ok?"

He licked her face again.

"Shhh, it's going to be alright." She wasn't sure if she was saying it to Sol or herself. Better to go with both.

A rung gave way beneath her foot half way down. Steph caught herself by painfully shoving her back against the wall of the shaft.

Sol began to bark like crazy.

"I'm okay Sol! It's…" she winced as she pulled her back off the wall, shifting her weight back onto the ladder despite its betrayal, "okay."

Sol stopped barking and Steph continued her descent.

The ladder held the rest of the way down.

She dropped to the ground, finding herself in a thin passage. It didn't feel like a proper part of the mine but neither was it entirely natural. It extended well beyond the reach of her torchlight into an indecipherable mess of diffused light.

Up until this point Sol had been her guide. Now that she had descended to a point he couldn't reach, she had no clear indication of where Flynn would have headed. If she headed off into the tunnel and it branched out in unknown directions, she may never find him. She would just have to hope Flynn left a trail like he had through the rest of the mine.

Steph was about to continue down the new tunnel but stopped, cocking her head. There was a… sound. Even in the dead silence of a million tonnes of earth and stone pressing down, it was barely audible.

She clicked the torch off. Having cut out the distraction of sight, she tried to focus more intently on the sound's source.

Instead of being lost in darkness with the torch now off, a weak line of purple light seeped out of a crack an arm's length away.

Flynn's black light. It had to be.

No longer questioning which direction to head, she pushed herself into the faintly lit crack.

On the other side, a gigantic amethyst coloured geode ensconced her. Crystals spiked up all over the floor, except at its very centre, where a pool of water glowed a soft purple. The light from the pool died, plunging the cavern into blackness before it rose again. It continued to pulse every few seconds.

She swept her torch across the concave ceiling, the crystals dazzling her with their scintillating refractions.

"Wow," she couldn't help whispering, her soft exclamation echoing all around her.

Steph refocused. Flynn.

If he had seen the same purple light she had, he would have investigated without a second thought. She had to check the entire cave before leaving.

She didn't have to search long.

"Oh God," Steph clamped both hands over her mouth, causing her to drop the torch.

Flynn was lying amongst the crystals jutting up from the floor. He didn't move. But something else did, barely visible amongst the purple atmosphere.

    Flynn was covered in a crawling mass of spiders.

16

"Flynn?"

He heard his name as if it came from the other side of a thick wall.

"Flynn."

Now the wall was getting thinner. Kind of like that motel they stopped over in when they were on that road trip last year and there had been a noisy couple on the other side.

"Flynn!"

Now there was no obstruction and he could identify the voice. Steph.

Steph. Down here, in the cave, when she was supposed to be at the cabin. He connected the dots. Sol must have brought her down here.

No longer unconscious, and remembering where he was, Flynn bolted upright. He was instantly struck back down by the pain of scores of needles jabbing into his entire body.

Steph screamed.

Oh God, the spiders.

"Steph." He had to talk around his tongue. Not a good sign. "Shine your light on me. It will scare them off."

Bright white light blinded him as Steph followed his instruction.

Flynn felt the fangs retract from his body as the spiders fled from the harsh light.

Steph rushed over and lifted him into a seated position.

His joints were stiff. Their venom had some sort of paralytic in it and he had been bitten by far more than one.

"Listen," he took a breath, trying to steady his voice, "listen to me. We've got to get me to a hospital. There's a specimen container," he stopped to breathe for a few seconds, "over there."

"But…" Steph was fearful, "how will they know what to do?"

She was, of course, referring to the fact that this was a previously undiscovered creature. There would be no anti-venom. He would be at the complete mercy of whatever toxicologist was nearby. But they were going to have to take that chance. A live specimen would increase the odds of that chance. If he was still conscious, he would try to help as best he could.

"Just get the container."

Steph rushed off in the direction he had indicated.

"There's nothing in here!" Steph shouted from the geode wall. She turned to face her husband and held up the sealed container, her torchlight shining through its plastic wall.

"What? Bring it here."

Sure enough, there was nothing inside. The spider had inexplicably vanished.

Flynn smiled.

"Why are you smiling?"

"What?" Flynn felt his face. He was smiling and he had no idea why. "The venom is a paralytic so–"

"How do you know that?"

Flynn flexed his arm painfully, "Sore joints."

"We've got to get you out of here."

"Soon…" Flynn was still inspecting the empty container, having taken the torch from his wife to do so.

"What do you mean 'soon'?" Steph was sounding frantic, "You've been bitten!"

Flynn found his black light and shone it inside the container.

The spider was suddenly visible, still sealed inside the container. He clicked the black light off and it disappeared.

"Oh God," Flynn's face was now fixed in a permanent smile but it couldn't hide the fear that filled his eyes, "Oh God."

"What?"

"The entire time I've been down here I've been using a black light. And then there's that–" he pointed at the pool "– which emits the same light."

"So what?"

"They're only visible under black light."

"You're telling me," Steph had to breathe for a few seconds, "these things are invisible?"

"Did you bring a black light?"

Steph shook her head, "Unlike you, it's not on the top of my packing list."

"Then this is all we've got," Flynn said, raising the small black cylinder in his hand. "It's the only way we're going to be able to see the spiders."

He shone it on the ground, revealing a throng of spiders that were closing in around them.

"Shine your torch!"

Steph whipped the white light over the floor and they disappeared from sight.

"Well this is going to be fun," Steph said sarcastically. "Now can we please get out of here?"

Flynn pulled his own white light from his pocket and clicked it on.

"These things have some sort of hive mentality." He created a pool of light around his feet. "They're working together. It's incredible." Even in their current plight, he couldn't turn off his inner arachnologist. "We need to stay in the torch light as much as we can. It's the only way we're going to avoid accidentally walking into them."

Flynn let out a small giggle.

Steph's voice was a horrified whisper, "Did… you just laugh?"

"No," Flynn giggled again, this time louder. His eyes widened, "What's happening?"

"Alright, we're moving," Steph said, grabbing Flynn and shining her torch downward as she moved for the crack.

"I was so close," Flynn said. Another giggle.

"You seriously need to stop doing that."

"I can't."

Steph didn't reply.

They reached the crack.

"Wait," Flynn stopped them and scoured the crack with the black light.

Both sides of it were coated in spiders. Every single eye was fixed on them, awaiting their next move.

"Ha," Flynn started to laugh, "Ha ha ha."

Steph hit him, "Stop."

"Ha ha ha ha ha ha ha," Flynn, through no choice of his own, ignored the request. A few seconds later he snapped out of it and he looked desperately at Steph, "I can't control it."

"If this wasn't so unfunny, I'd tell you that you look exactly like the Joker."

"You did just tell me," Flynn said, grinning.

Steph ignored him and shone her torch at the base of the crack, engulfing its lower reaches with the bright white light. Although they couldn't see it, they heard the spiders scurrying away from the light as she worked it higher and higher up the crack.

She reached head height and pushed Flynn into the crack,

"Go go!"

He obeyed and Steph followed behind, still shining the light above them to ward off their invisible assailants.

"Oh boy," Flynn said.

He was wielding a torch in either hand. One purple and the other white. With a rapid interchanging of light, he kept a mass of spiders between them and the ladder both visible and at bay.

"Keep moving," Steph ordered.

"It's hard to move…" Flynn said, cracking his neck.

"That's why we need to keep moving… Please."

Trading visibility for passage, Flynn trained the light on the ladder and Steph kept their feet clear.

"Sol's at the top waiting for us," she said.

Sol obviously heard the mention of his name and let out a series of frantic barks and snarls followed by what could only be described as a canine shriek.

Steph and Flynn shared a look. They had never heard him make that sound before.

They rushed up the ladder.

17

Sol was still and trembling when they arrived at the top of the ladder. Seeing Flynn and Steph, he began to whimper. He was visibly fighting the instinct to run.

"Stay very still Sol," Flynn said softly, fighting off a laugh. He shone the black light on him, revealing what he dreaded.

The German Shepherd was coated in spiders.

The sight of the spiders covering him caused Sol to panic and he could stay still no longer, snapping at the creatures.

"Sol no!" Steph screamed.

He let out another canine shriek as the spiders began to bite him, latching on with their monstrous leg-ensconced fangs. Sol tried to tear them off in a frenzy, drawing blood.

Steph shone her torch onto Sol, causing the spiders to disappear from sight. But Sol continued to tear, subjecting them to the sight of their beloved pet ripping at his fur and flesh with his own sharp teeth.

Despite witnessing such a horrific sight, Flynn could hold himself back no longer. He burst into a fit of air sucking laughter, his cackle not unlike the comic book character Steph had compared him to only a minute ago. Trying to stop the involuntary laughter, he grabbed at his stomach.

The black light smashed on the ground.

Sol joined Flynn's laughter with his own, chilling version. Half howl, half wheeze, Sol fell to the ground and thrashed around.

Tears welled in Steph's eyes as she watched her husband and dog subjected to the effects of the spiders' venom but it didn't stop her from taking action.

Hoping against hope that the white light was still having the same effect on the spiders, she frantically swept it over Sol. Trusting the light had done its job, and with no way to check now that the black light had smashed, she grabbed Sol and hefted him up into her arms.

The heavy animal bucked in her arms, spasming with the forced laughter coursing through his body. Steph held her head back, avoiding his snapping jaws as he tried to control himself. Blood splashed crimson against her jacket.

"Flynn," she could barely speak, "I need you to follow me."

Her husband had also fallen to the ground and was writhing in his laughter. He looked up at her, terror in his eyes. Between chuckles he managed to say, "I… I can't."

Steph realised the choice she had to make, one she didn't even need to deliberate over. Neither Sol or Flynn could move without her help. She wasn't going to be able to save them both.

She set Sol down on the ground and hoisted Flynn's arm over her shoulders, lifting him up in the process.

"Can you shine your torch?" she asked as he guffawed loudly into her ear. She could hear thousands of legs scurrying around them. They weren't getting out of here easy, that was sure.

"Y-yes…" Flynn managed to wheeze, "I think so."

"Good," she forced the torch into his hand, closing his fingers over it, "Don't let go."

They hobbled along the passage, sweeping their torches all around.

Flynn's laughter continued to intensify. The light of his torch wheeled around them in a crazy, jerky display.

"What about Sol?" He managed to gasp.

Steph refused to answer that question, keeping her eyes ahead except for the occasional torch shine behind them from her own light. The sounds of Sol's laughter echoed after them.

She spotted a chocolate bar by a corner and turned them down the new passage, retracing the route Flynn had mapped out earlier.

They soon arrived at the crack between the mine and the cavern. Steph quickly swept both torches through the crack and pushed Flynn ahead of her, hoping against hope that any spiders that might be ahead of them had fled as she had scoured the crack with light.

As they hobbled across the open expanse of the cavern, dodging the kangaroo carcasses, Sol let out a series of gut wrenching shrieks that echoed up through the mine, breaking the horrific sounds of his canine laughter. Moments later he fell silent.

Steph burst into tears, "I'm sorry Sol, I'm so so sorry."

She almost dropped Flynn as he slumped unconscious, cutting off his own creepy laughter.

Fuelled by adrenaline and desperation, she hoisted him over her shoulders. Thank God he wasn't that much bigger than she was. Still, carrying him wasn't easy. She was going to give him so much crap for this… in time.

Steph moved as quickly as she could through the rest of the mine, painfully aware of the fact she could now hear thousands of scurrying feet behind her. Somehow she managed to shine one torch forward and the other backward. She just hoped it was enough to keep the spiders away.

She pushed Flynn through the final crack, trying not to bang his head against the rough stone walls. Forgetting its depth, she almost dropped Flynn on his face as they suddenly spilled out into the cellar.

Steph hoisted him back onto her shoulders, feeling her muscles scream beneath the strain. Almost there. She just had to get up the cellar stairs and back to the caravan park. She would call an ambulance the moment she was out of the shed and had reception.

An idea hit her.

It was dark outside and she had no idea if the spiders would continue to pursue them beyond the cave. Her energy was fading fast and she wasn't sure how quickly she could continue to move. If the spiders caught up they would both suffer the same fate as Sol. She had to stop them in their tracks.

Careful not to drop Flynn and using the wall to support her, she snatched up Flynn's bag.

She shoved one of the torches into her mouth and tossed the other into the crack, flooding all but its upper reaches with light. The spiders would soon figure out how to reach them so she had to move quickly.

She unzipped the front pocket of the bag and retrieved a lighter. Years ago – before they began dating – Flynn had been a smoker. Then they started going out and she had made him quit. It must have been love because he ditched the cigarettes within a week. Cold turkey.

Despite quitting, his lighter had remained. Flynn held that it had use beyond lighting 'sticks of smoky death'. Yes, she had once been a pretentious English major just like her students.

Right now, she couldn't be more grateful that he still kept it.

Still holding onto the bag, she climbed the cellar stairs to the shed above. Every step caused her muscles to scream louder and louder. She was going to collapse soon.

She had to get back to the caravan park. Then she could collapse.

Bursting out of the shed, she almost tripped over the chain lying in the undergrowth.

Steph dumped Flynn on the ground, no longer caring how many bruises he woke up with, if he woke up at all…

No! She couldn't think like that. Not now. She was almost there.

Unable to lock the shed with a broken chain and padlock, Steph pulled the doors close together and tried to prevent them swinging back and forth. Anything to slow them down before they found the cracks and crevices that would allow them to burst forth into the wider world.

She was aware she was making them more monstrous and calculating in her mind than their animal instincts would allow but she didn't care. They had killed their dog, and they might have killed her husband. They were murderous monsters in her mind.

Phone in one hand and lighter in the other, she set fire to the dead overgrowth covering the shed. Hungry for flame, the collection of dead leaves, twigs and creeping foliage erupted in plumes of gold and orange.

The emergency call connected. She didn't bother listening to the menu and screamed into the device, "Ambulance!"

A few seconds later she was connected to an operator. She treated the living person with the same tone, "I need an ambulance as quickly as possible!"

"Ma'am, I need you to calm down."

"My husband has been bitten by…" she tried to think, "I don't know how many spiders. I need an ambulance. And I need it now!"

"Where are you?"

"Blue Mountains Caravan Park, Katoomba, New South Wales."

"Ma'am, do you know the exact address?"

"No! I–" Steph tried to steady her voice, "I don't."

"It's okay. An ambulance is on its way. Can you stay on the line?"

Steph didn't bother replying, pocketing the device while remaining on the call so she could lift Flynn back onto her shoulders.

The caravan park. She had to make it to the caravan park. Then she could collapse. Then her job was done.

She staggered through the bush as quickly as she could, a shadow cast before them by the flickering of the flames and horrors they left behind.

It didn't take long for her to reach the edge of the caravan park. Blue and red lights were already there to greet her.

She summoned the last reserves of her strength. Tears of fear, pain, and exhaustion were streaking down her face by the time she met the paramedics and collapsed, her husband's body on top of her.

18

Flynn stood in the backyard, staring at the crude wooden cross poking up out of the garden, a small mound in front of it.

They had no body to bury, so small parts of Sol's life lay beneath the cross. His leash. His favourite ball. A packet of jerky. All things he had loved.

Tears slipped down Flynn's cheeks.

He heard the back door open and close. Moments later Steph's hand was around his waist.

For the first few days after their tragic trip into the mine, Flynn had been hospitalized and in a coma. Thankfully the spiders' venom hadn't proved fatal, even in the large amounts that had been injected into Flynn's body. It was simply a form of liquid anaesthetic designed to immobilize prey. The doctor's prescription had taken the form of close examination as the venom worked its way out of Flynn's system. Except for the days of unconsciousness, the simplicity of Flynn's recovery had been such a relief.

Although, this knowledge was also sobering: Sol was a large dog and the venom wouldn't have been enough to kill him either.

Steph remembered how he had ripped at his own body as the spiders crawled over him and was unable to contain a sob as she stood over the grave of remembrance.

Flynn pulled her closer, letting her bury her head in his shoulder.

His phone buzzed but he didn't bother checking it, knowing exactly what the screen would tell him.

Over the past few weeks, Isaac had sent him message after message, email after email, phone call after phone call. Flynn hadn't answered a single one. He felt like the teen was owed an explanation… some small window into what had happened down in that mine. But Flynn hadn't been able to think of a way to encapsulate the mystery and horror of what they had experienced.

Instead, he had abandoned any dreams of scientific glory. The spiders they had found didn't exist, at least that's what Flynn would say. Or maybe he would tell him it did exist but it wasn't a new species? It was an extremely rare spider? Nothing special. Nothing new. Nothing worth remembering. And yet, Flynn would remember them for the rest of his life.

He pulled away from Steph and began drafting a message: *Checked things out and found that it's nothing special. It's actually an obscure species of cave spider that isn't found too often. Sorry to get your hopes up but it's not a new species. It's just rare.*

He handed the device to his wife. She read it over before deleting the entire thing. She wrote something far more succinct and final.

The Isaac Spider doesn't exist. Forget about it.

She hit send.

THE END

ACKNOWLEDGEMENTS

Marcus for introducing me to the possibilities of self-publishing.

Lexia for helping me polish the final version of 'The Isaac Spiders'.

Karl for insights into the world of self-publishing and bookselling.

Tom for making sure this print version wasn't a horrible mess.

My parents for never once believing I was anything but a writer.

Kira, my wife, who has helped dreams become reality ever since I met her.

And to you, my readers, for joining me on this journey.

ABOUT THE AUTHOR

Thomas Rose lives in Canberra, Australia with his wife Kira. As well as being a self-published author of thriller and dystopian fiction, he spends his time as an English tutor and communications expert. When he isn't writing, he's either rock climbing or wandering the streets late at night, searching for the next piece of inspiration.

If you want to get in touch with Thomas, or read any of his other stories, visit him at www.Thomas-Rose.com.

www.ingramcontent.com/pod-product-compliance
Lightning Source LLC
Chambersburg PA
CBHW070316120726
47910CB00007B/2502